Robbie's Rac

by Peter R Peake

When Flash (Farmer Giles' new car) arrives in Farmer James'
yard, this leads to a quarrel. Flash challenges Robbie to a race
and pride comes before a fall.

Robbie was just taking a well-earned rest, only to be woken by the noise of a loud throaty engine, followed by a screech of brakes, as a long, low, red sports car pulled up by his side. The door opened and out stepped Farmer Giles who walked off to find Farmer James.

"And who are you?" Robbie asked.

"I'm Flash, Farmer Giles' new car."

"Well, you're not very suitable, are you?"

"What do you mean NOT SUITABLE?"

"You're not a farmer's car, are you?"

"NOT A FARMER'S CAR? Anyone who owns me has such pride. I am a status symbol," Flash said.

"You're still no use to a farmer," Robbie replied.

"All right, tell me what you can do that I can't."

"Well, for a start you're too small, only a two-seater."

"I'm not" Flash replied. "I'm a four-seater. Mr and Mrs Giles sit in the front and Nell and Neil in the back."

"But they're dogs" Robbie replied.

"So two humans, two dogs. What's the difference, a four-seater?"

Robbie would have said that dogs don't count, only he could see Defa and Deli coming across the yard to look at Farmer Giles' new car and he didn't want to upset them.

"The truth is, Farmer James is just a STICK IN THE MUD: he doesn't move with the times. Speed is what counts now. Why, I'm so fast, sometimes I arrive before I've even started." Flash gave his engine a throaty roar just to make the point.

"STUCK IN THE MUD. That's just what you would be if you worked on a farm," Robbie told Flash. He was starting to get fed up with Flash's self-importance.

"I can go anywhere a Farm Ranger can."

"No, you can't."

"Yes, I can. Just watch this!" Flash pressed a button, and slowly his body started to rise off the ground, and down came his wheels. "Now you can see: I'm built to go over any ground. Wet or dry. Fast or slow."

Robbie looked at him. "You're not a Farm Ranger."

"I might not be a Farm Ranger" said Flash. "But I can go anywhere you can at twice - no four times the speed, and I'm comfortable to drive, and to prove it I'll race you around the farm any day, anywhere. You can pick the route."

Robbie knew Flash was starting to get a little silly now. *"How do you know I won't pick a route you can't follow?"* Robbie asked.

"Impossible - only you will be following me."

"All right, tomorrow at 12, in the farm yard"

The next day, all was ready. Robbie and Flash lined up side by side. Solomon was going to fire the starting gun and be the time-keeper. *"You have 35 minutes to complete the race,"* he bleated.

"NO, that means Robbie has 35 minutes. I only need 15", said Flash.

"Are the dogs in place to see fair play?"

It had been arranged Defa and Deli would travel with Flash and Nell and Neil with Robbie. Solomon looked in each vehicle to check the dogs were there.

BANG! They were off. Flash was away with a hail of stones torn out of the road as his wheels accelerated at such speed that his body could hardly take the pace. Soon all you could see was his dust in the distance.

Robbie glided away after him with Nell and Neil. *"This isn't right"* Nell said. *"These races are silly. Flash will win and then he will be even more arrogant."*

"You are right Nell, he will be even worse" Neil added. *"You should not have agreed to this race Robbie."*

Robbie said nothing. He just kept speeding down the farm road, onto the highway. Then back on to Farmer James' land and down to the river. The corn had been harvested and Farmer James had started to plough the field.

Robbie had been speaking to Terry Tractor. He knew every inch of the farmland and they had hatched up a plot between them.

"Slow down, you're throwing us from side to side" Defa barked at Flash as his head hit the roof again.

"I said I'd do it in 15 minutes and we've been 9 already, that's only 6 left. I'll go slower over the ploughed ground."

Defa sat up with alarm. *"You're not going to drive over the ploughed ground in this car? Surely not? Even a Farm Ranger would find it difficult."*

"Fiddle-de-dee - just watch me!" With that, Flash accelerated even more. The trap was set and he was going to jump right into it with all four tyres. This was what Robbie had planned.

He knew Flash was far faster than he was, so something was needed to slow him down.

"There's a patch of low lying ground down by the river that floods and is still very wet, Terry Tractor had told Robbie. *"I nearly got stuck in it when we were ploughing the field."*

"That's perfect" Robbie said. *"Please don't plough around the outside of the field."*

"Okay, I'll leave it for now."

Robbie was jogging along at his top speed way behind. Flash had passed over the fields that led to the river and the wet patch, and with a roar from his engine he started to cross it.

"*You stupid car!*" Deli barked as the mud flew off Flash's back wheels, as he accelerated more and more.

"*I'm stuck, I'm stuck!*" Flash cried as he changed from reverse to forward gears, but it was no use. No matter how much he shunted to and fro, the car only sank deeper into the wet mud, and that was that.

Just then Robbie appeared. *"I just knew it!"* he said as he looked at Flash, stuck in the wet patch. Any sensible car would have driven around the ploughed ground, but not Flash. He'd just had to show off. *"WELL NOW HE'S STUCK!"*

"Pull me out, pull me out!" Flash cried.

"Not likely, I'll lose the race if I stop to pull you out." Robbie carefully drove around the outside of the wet ploughed ground and was soon back in the farmyard.

"29 and a half minutes and you are the winner" Solomon announced.

"What about Flash?" Nell asked.

"We'll send Terry down to the river with a big chain to pull him out."

When Flash did finally arrive back in the yard Nell had something to say to him. "Just look at you covered with mud from tyre to roof! I shouldn't tell Farmer Giles you've been out by yourself on this silly prank. He won't be pleased and he'll probably cut your petrol allowance."

"Yes, yes this is all very silly. I should go down to the pond and get the ducks to clean you" Solomon added.

Robbie looked very satisfied with himself. It had been a fair race and he had won. Until Solomon turned to him. *"I don't think Farmer James would be too pleased with you either if he knew you've been out racing around the farm by yourself."*

Robbie quietly slipped behind him into his garage and closed the door, and murmered *"good night"*. It had been a good day.

The End

New series of books for younger readers

Snowy's Lapland Adventure
Solomon's Birthday Meal
Farmer James Counting Book

Coming Soon
Mrs James' Sofa

Twinkle and Twilight
Daisy's Birthday
Save Christmas

Coming Soon
A Royal Visit

Part of the Farmer James series

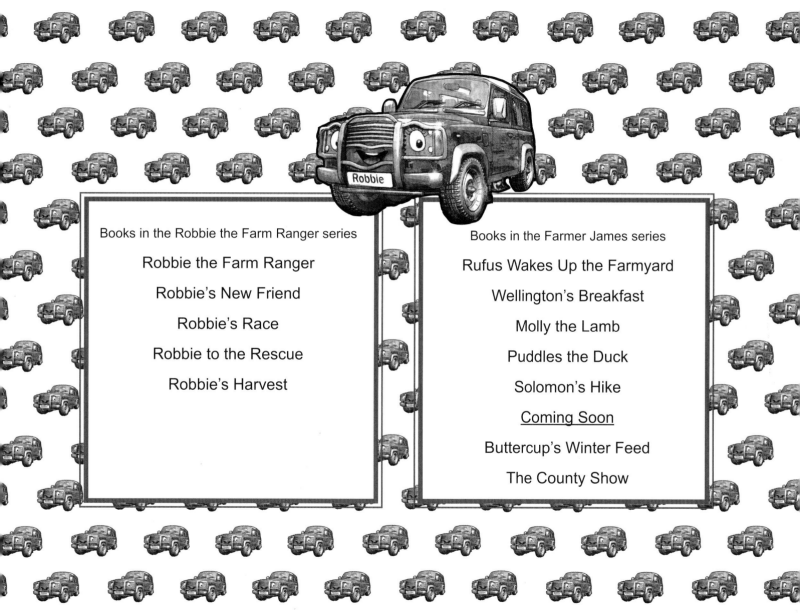

Books in the Robbie the Farm Ranger series

Robbie the Farm Ranger

Robbie's New Friend

Robbie's Race

Robbie to the Rescue

Robbie's Harvest

Books in the Farmer James series

Rufus Wakes Up the Farmyard

Wellington's Breakfast

Molly the Lamb

Puddles the Duck

Solomon's Hike

<u>Coming Soon</u>

Buttercup's Winter Feed

The County Show

FLASH is a copy of my 1986 Porsche 924S - my pride and joy. It was developed by Porsche for Volkswagen as a budget luxury sports car, to the extent that VW used readily available parts, including a souped-up engine from one of their existing vans. It became known as "the Sport's Car with a van engine". The next time there is a Classic Car rally in your area see if you can spot one of these cars.